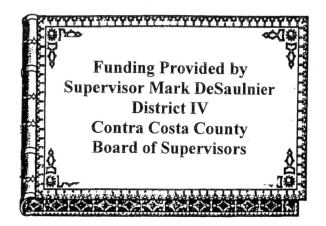

Funding Provided by
Supervisor Mark DeSaulnier
District IV
Contra Costa County
Board of Supervisors

whose mouse are you?

BY ROBERT KRAUS • PICTURES BY JOSE ARUEGO

Aladdin Paperbacks

First Aladdin Paperbacks edition 1986
Revised format edition 1998

Aladdin Paperbacks
An imprint of Simon & Schuster Children's Publishing Division
1230 Avenue of the Americas
New York, NY 10020

Manufactured in China
36 35 34 33 32 31 30

Library of Congress Cataloging-in-Publication Data

Kraus, Robert, 1925–
   Whose mouse are you?

   Reprint. Originally published; New York: Collier
Books, 1972 c1970.
   Summary: A lonely little mouse has to be resourceful
in order to bring his family back together.
   [1. Mice—Fiction.   2. Stories in rhyme]
I. Aruego, José, ill.   II. Title.
PZ8.3.K864Wh   1986   [E]   86-16376
ISBN-13: 978-0-689-71142-8 (Aladdin pbk.)
ISBN-10: 0-689-71142-5 (Aladdin pbk.)

For Bruce and Billy

Whose mouse are you?

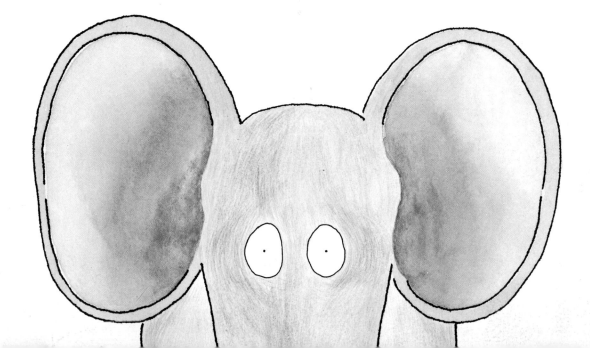

Nobody's mouse.

Where is your mother?

Inside the cat.

Where is your father?

Caught in a trap.

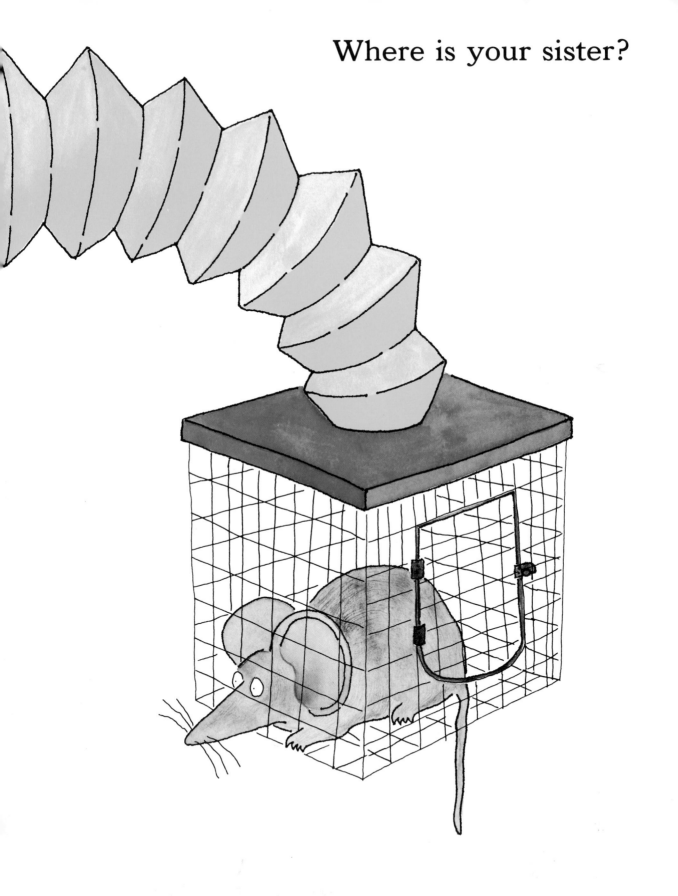

Where is your sister?

Far from home.

your brother?

I have none.

What will you do?

Shake my mother out of the cat!

Free my father from the trap!

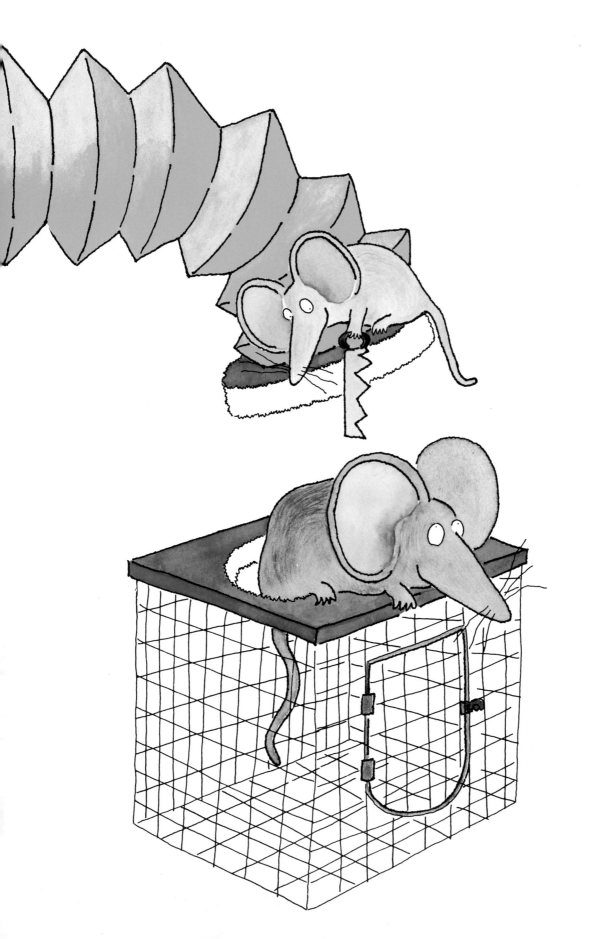

Find my sister and bring her home.

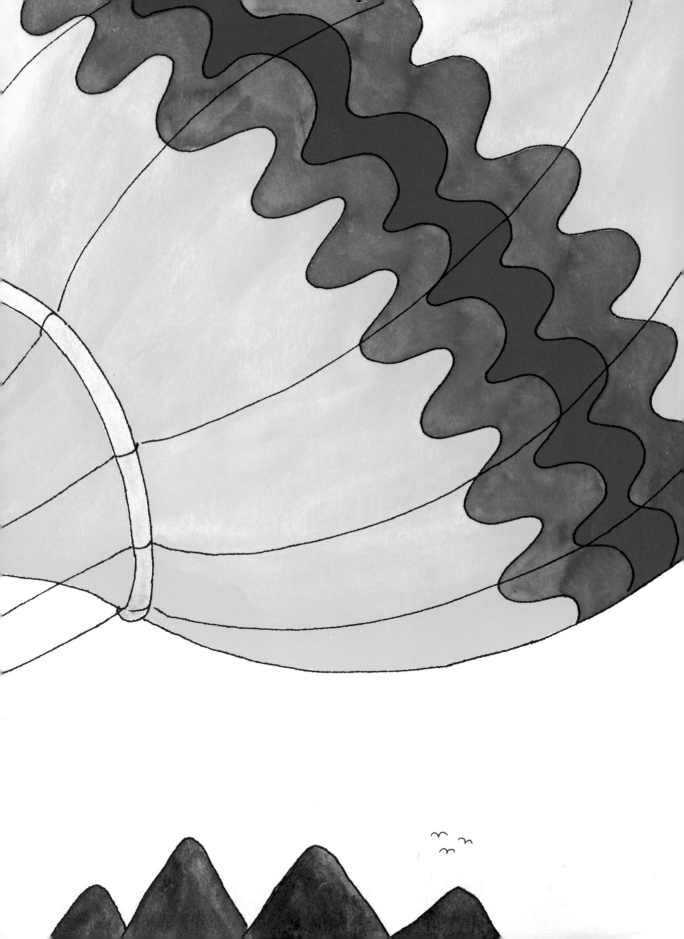

Wish for a brother as I have none.

Now whose mouse are you?

My mother's mouse, she loves me so.

My father's mouse, from head to toe.

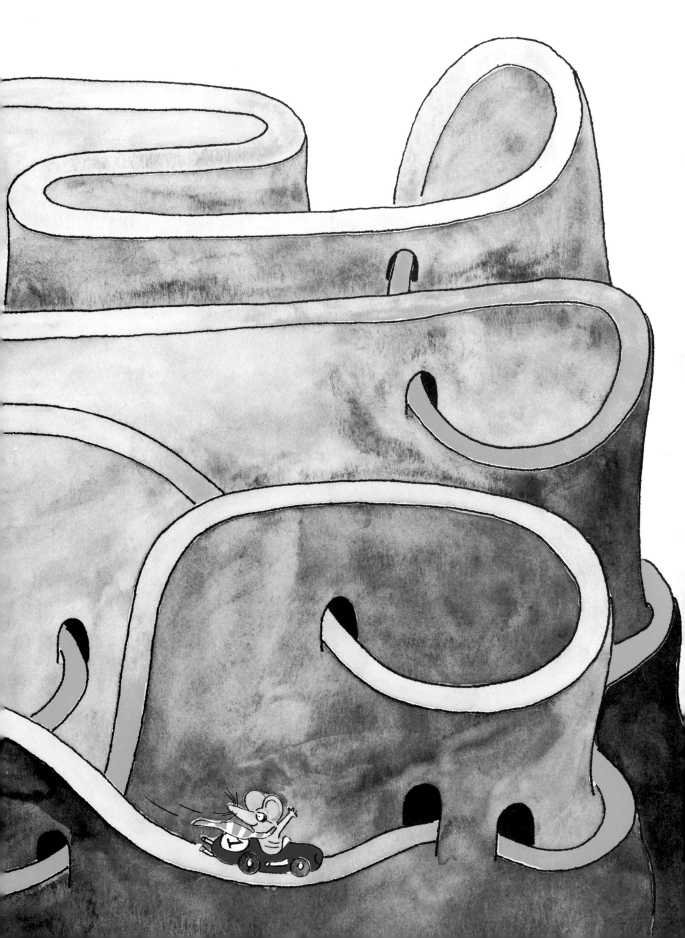

My sister's mouse, she loves me too.

My brother's mouse. . . .

Your brother's mouse?

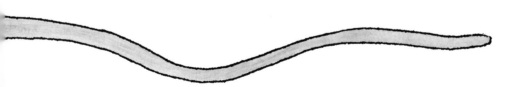

My brother's mouse—he's *brand* new!